SAVE THE CROWS

BY
GEORGE KOSANA

Burning Bulb

PUBLISHING

Save the Crows by **George Kosana**
Copyright © 2001 George Kosana. All rights reserved.
2014 Special Edition produced by Burning Bulb Publishing
P.O. Box 4721, Bridgeport, WV 26330.
Cover designed by Gary Lee Vincent with images licensed from
fotolia.com (46245194 & 52790556).
ISBN: 978-0692219799

None of us know anything is wrong with Roger. Sure, he's a lousy card player. Whenever he has a good hand his eyes light up like a Christmas tree, and he gets abnormally silent. He might as well announce his good fortune over a loud speaker. But, being a poor gambler doesn't mean you're insane, and I know him better than any poker player at this table. We went through high school together, graduated in 1950, and Korea is seven years behind me.

Roger asks about crow hunting. I begin telling him the how's and where's when the dealer interrupts. "You two gonna hunt crows or play poker?" I swig on my sixth beer and toss in the ante. Roger stands, searches his pockets, and asks, "Do you guys really get paid to hunt crows?"

The dealer speaks before I answer, "Either ante up, or drop." I concentrate on the cards. Several hands are played before I notice Roger is gone and I had forgotten to answer his question. I call a bet. I think I have a straight. I don't, the nine is missing. I realize my mistake. It's time to quit. I pick up my winnings and head for the hotel. It's three o'clock in the morning and I need sleep. My car bounces off the curb when I pull in.

A thought occurs to me, booze does impair your judgment. In the room I'm under the covers and asleep almost immediately.

"GENE KARNES! GET UP! IT'S ME, ROGER DANTZ! IT'S TIME TO GO CROW HUNTING!"

Heavy banging on the door, accompanied by a loud voice, jars me out of a sound sleep. There is a pause, then it starts again, only this time it might as well be the big bass drum in a marching band at a Saturday afternoon football game. The walls rattle. My head throbs in rhythm with the pounds.

Hotel tenants up and down both sides of the hallway shout protests over this intrusion. Muffled voices pour out from behind each closed door, "KEEP THE NOISE DOWN!""HEY, I'M TRYING TO GET SOME SLEEP!""WE COULD USE SOME PEACE AND QUIET AROUND HERE!"

They reflect my sentiments exactly, but Roger persists. This time he hits the door so hard my bed vibrates. I resent being forced out from under the warm covers and my head aches. I fling the blankets aside, feel both my feet find their way to the floor, and stand.

Groggy, and only half awake, I shuffle across the cool surface of the linoleum and come to a stop in front of the offending wooden rectangle. Both of my hands search for, and find, the knobs on the locks. I turn each until the click of metal signals they are open. The dead bolt slides back and I allow the owner of that outrageous voice to enter. At least other tenants will get some sleep. Letting him in will prove to be a mistake, a very serious mistake. "C'mon! Let's go! It's Saturday morning!" He hands me a paper cup full of hot coffee. It slops over the rim of the container and the steaming brew runs down my fingers. Suddenly, I am awake.

"It's ten-thirty. You promised to take me crow hunting today. Let's go!"

Promise? I remember no promise. I try to shake off my hangover. I can't recall telling him we'd hunt today. For some strange reason I stare at him. Now, maybe for the first time, I'm thinking there always was something a little different about the guy, something you couldn't quite put your finger on, later this day that strangeness would explode and in a most terrifying way.

The hand that holds the coffee cup points across the room. My head kicks, screams, and resists being returned to a full level of consciousness. "A shotgun and a canvas bag with shells are in the closet."

My other hand sweeps across the desk and scoops up a set of keys. I offer them to him. "Put everything in the trunk of the car while I wash up."

I fix the lock so the door stays open, grab my shaving kit, a towel, the coffee, and head for the community bathroom at the end of the hall. It is occupied. I finish the hot brew while I wait my turn.

Thump. Thump. The stock of my twelve gauge bounces off each stile in the railing of the wooden banister on its way outside. Roger doesn't even know how to carry a weapon. Through the fog my head screams, "What am I getting myself into?" I should recognize the signs, call off the hunt, and the day, but for reasons I can't explain, I don't. The room finally empties and it's my turn.

A face heavily lathered in shaving cream, stares back at me through the mirror mounted above the sink. The safety razor drags across a section of cheek. It carves a path through the soap, clips into the basin full of hot water, and rinses clean. My mind drifts back to a time that seems centuries ago, our high school days.

We were in the same classes from the seventh to the twelfth grades. Roger and I played for a sandlot baseball team. He was the third baseman, and l was behind the plate. The catcher. Now that I think about it, I liked fast action. Excitement. I still do. Before this day ends I will have my full share of both.

Roger met Sally Johnson during one of our games. It was instant romance. They were smitten with each other and soon became high school sweethearts. They have been together ever since. We double-dated a few times.

Everyone notices how delightfully happy they are. They fully enjoy each shared moment and light up any room they enter. It's funny the way things happen. The entire school, myself included, expected them to marry. Somehow it hasn't happened, at least not yet.

Finished washing and back in the room, I pull on my loose fitting camouflage pants and shirt. The specialty clothing must fit loosely to avoid restricting movements and help break up the silhouette outline of the body. Heavy socks adorn each foot and the calf high leather hunting boots lace up quickly. The whole thing is topped off with my matching hunting hat. One day I'm going to wash it, but not today.

I reach around behind me until my fingers touch the piece of plastic pinned to the shirt in the center of the back. My hunting license hangs in place. I am ready. Preoccupied with where we will hunt, and still not completely rid of my hangover, I fail to take notice of the trousers I wore last night. They hang draped over a chair. I leave the room without even looking at them. Another mistake I will come to regret.

Roger stands alongside the car dressed in street clothes. That's odd. "Where's your stuff? You lock it in the trunk?" For some reason his answer doesn't surprise me.

"I don't have any. This is a trial run for me, remember?"

It hits me, "That's right. You don't hunt." I retrieve the keys and unlock the car. We both get in. "Don't expect too much. It's a good hour's ride to the farm road, then another twenty minutes or so to the section we hunt, and it will take time to get set up."

I'm guessing he will watch me to learn how it's done. One thing is certain; I won't let him fire a single shot until after he buys his hunting license. The engine roars to life and the emergency brake releases. The gearshift lever slides into drive two, and we pull away. "Personally I think we're wasting our time. What the hell, at least you're enthusiastic."

Still trying to shake off the effect of the booze I don't even notice Roger hasn't answered me. He stares at each building we pass as though it's the first time he's ever laid eyes on one.

I continue, "Crows are very smart birds. They have tremendous survival instincts and great eyesight. Believe it or not, they can spot the reflections off the metal hinges on a pair of eyeglasses from more than a hundred yards away, and when they do, they'll immediately veer off, and won't come into shotgun range. How do you expect to conceal yourself when you don't even have camouflage clothing?"

The direct question brings him back from that private place his mind visits. I toss my hat onto the rear seat. "You don't even have a shotgun. What are you going to do, throw stones at them?"

He shifts uneasily in the seat. His demeanor suggests that remark has wounded him slightly. It appears he is preparing an answer but never offers it. He stares out the window; his mind is a million miles away.

I sympathize with him. There are times when I wish people I happen to be with would just shut up, leave me, and my thoughts alone, and quit bothering me. Why should he be any different? Something else troubles me. I can't identify it. A thought tries to creep through the cobwebs but isn't able to break free. I can't recognize it, categorize it, confront it, or resolve it. Whatever it was, it's gone. It retreats into the haze of my hangover. Perhaps I still feel the effect of too little sleep, too much poker, and way too much beer.

Roger's unexpected intrusion has left me feeling uneasy and I can't understand why. I have no idea what is coming. If I did perhaps I would be able to prepare myself for it, but I don't think anyone really could.

Roger returns for a moment. "This trip is just to show me how it's done. If I like it, then I will buy the equipment I need, and take up the sport. Does this farmer really pay you guys to hunt his farm and shoot crows?"

"Ten cents per bird. He hopes we bring him bushels full of dead crows each time we hunt. He is disappointed if we don't have at least five kills apiece. This farmer told us he planted one section of corn three times in the same year. Crows scavenged the plot and picked it clean every time. He never realized so much as a single ear of corn from that field the entire year. As far as he is concerned, he'd like to see them all killed off. I haven't had this much shooting since I was in the Marine Corps in Korea. Those dimes add up and it pays for our ammunition."

We reach the intersection at the state highway and turn onto the road that leads to his farm. Traffic begins to thin out as we put the city behind us. An occasional car passes and we approach a service plaza.

Approximately a hundred yards ahead a motorcycle rider signals he intends to turn into the gas station. We have plenty of room, but instinctively I back off the pedal. I glance at the fuel gauge. It hovers between the three quarter mark and full.

The two wheeled machine starts into the turn. For reasons unknown, the rider misjudges the maneuver. He misses the entrance ramp by several feet. The front wheel of his machine plows head on into the side of the high walled curb. The bike pitches sideways and the rider is thrown. He lands on his back, slides, skids, and rolls across the pavement before he slams into the pump islands.

The rider-less motorcycle caroms off the curb. Somehow it stays upright and wobbles across the asphalt before it finally topples over and comes to rest in the middle of the passing lane. We are well behind the accident.

Two customers run out. They dart across the lot out onto the highway. They lift the fallen motorcycle and push it off the road back into the plaza. Luckily traffic is light. They manage to do it without another accident.

Others attend to the fallen rider. They have him on his feet. His gestures indicate he is more embarrassed than hurt. His concerns are for his machine, and not for himself. The small crowd has everything under control, so we continue on our way.

Roger leans his head out of the Opening, and takes several deep breaths. He sits back and lights up a king-size, filtered, Marlboro cigarette. He drags heavily on it and draws the smoke deep into his lungs.

He follows a ritual he often practices to relax, to calm himself, and regain control of his situation. In a normal voice he says something odd, "Some people live in a tree. I live in a rotten log."

I don't understand what he means by that remark. The inflection, and the tone in which it is said sends a chill up my spine. The hair on the back of my neck rises and I get an uneasy feeling.

He continues. "Sally broke up with me three weeks and two days ago. We're finished Last night, I lose a hundred and fifty dollars playing poker with you guys, and now I have a ringside seat and get to watch some clown dump his bike."

He strikes the dashboard, viciously flicks ashes from his cigarette, and stomps the floor. I wait. He usually follows a tirade with a cynical remark. That's his style. This time he doesn't. He slouches down deep into the seat, sweats, and stares straight ahead. He is visibly upset and never smiles.

I glance at the center of the dashboard. The clock hands point straight up. "Twelve o'clock! It's twelve o'clock! You said it was ten thirty."

A few seconds pass. He looks at his wristwatch. "I lied." He continues to stare straight ahead. Suddenly he blurts out, "Always! Always! Always! I lose at poker. I always lose. I have no luck with cards."

I make a mistake and criticize him. "You always tip off your hand Roger."

"What!" he shouts, "I'm the best player in the game." I never tip my hand. When I do get good cards I keep absolutely quiet about it. Mostly, I get dealt garbage. I'm not lucky like you."

I force back the temptation to tell him, when you do get totally quiet and wide-eyed is when... what's the use of explaining? I shut up and drive.

A sense of humor helps everyone through rough times. I recall the ninth grade. We were both educated in the unpaved alleyway behind our school where we were introduced to gambling. During the recess periods many students would congregate there and shoot dice or play poker. Any game was fine with us. We didn't know what we were doing, but we were eager to learn.

In one particular spree that spanned three consecutive weeks we lost every penny we had between us. On the last day of that binge I am flat broke when the bell rings and signals classes are about to resume.

The game breaks up. Roger looks into the palm of his hand. He holds a hot nickel. He stares at it for a moment, tosses it onto the roof of the school building and says," They need it more than I do." We laughed, and went without another lunch. It was then we agreed, if we are going to gamble, we better learn how to do it.

That's the Roger I remember, carefree and happy-go-lucky. We arrive at another intersection and traffic light. "Here's where we turn. Twenty-five minutes more and we're at the farm."

"Don't make the turn. Get in the far left lane and take that road instead." It is a command more than it is a request and it catches me off guard. His voice is louder than it should be and has an edge to it. "Hang a left. We won't hunt. This'll take us to Shawnee Creek State Park. That's where I really want to go. There's something there I want to see."

I look at him. "Shawnee? That's quite a ride Roger. We don't have enough gas for a round trip. Besides, it's already after noon. It gets dark around five-thirty, or six o'clock at this time of year. They'll be closed by the time we get there."

He stares straight ahead and doesn't smile. His hands clench into tight fists. His knuckles are white. He fires up another king sized, filtered, Marlboro. This time he smokes out of desperation. He turns the radio on and tunes it to a station. "Go to Shawnee." He turns the volume up so loud the noise hurts my ears. He screams to be heard over it. "GO TO SHAWNEE!"

This time it cannot be misinterpreted. He issued me an order. I can't explain why, but I carry it out. I swing the car into the left lane, signal my turn, and wait for the light. Maybe somewhere deep down inside I don't really want to take him hunting. We're through the tum and I reach across to lower the sound. Roger stops me.

Aggressively, he pushes my hand aside. It is more of a threatening gesture than a defensive move. He defies me to turn down my own radio. If I want the volume lowered, I'll lower it.

I reach for the control knob a second time. He swats my hand away. "THIS IS GETTING A LITTLE STRANGE ROGER!" Again, I reach for the volume, and again, he stops me.

"SOME PEOPLE LIVE IN A TREE! I LIVE IN A ROTTEN LOG! Then almost as an afterthought he cries out, "BESIDES, LOOK AT ALL THE CROWS I'M SAVING!" His eyes glaze over. His features contort somewhat. An odd look registers across his face.

Somehow his mind equates not hunting the birds with some worthwhile meaningful accomplishment, as though he has achieved some noble purpose, gained some elusive goal. The tone in his voice reveals he is proud of that fact. A contest of wills begins.

I move for the radio. He reacts, and pushes me away. This time I exert force and succeed in knocking his hand aside. I win, and finally reduce the noise to a reasonable level. He slumps in his seat, defeated. He stares straight ahead, and pouts.

I argue with myself as I drive. Why am I doing this? Why am I here? I have no answer. It's as though some unexplainable force guides me, wills me to see this through, It makes no sense, but I continue to drive in spite of myself. Roger sits and stares. He smokes one cigarette after another.

Miles melt away, and while he looks directly out the window, he fails to notice them pass. There is no conversation. He seems to be in a strange trance.

At four forty-five in the afternoon I speak out "We're here buddy"

The announcement jolts Roger back. He sits upright and leans forward. He focuses his attention on the surroundings. I slow down. We approach the park entrance and I glance at the gas gauge. The needle sits just under the quarter tank mark.

Completely alert, he points "Pull into the main parking lot and drive through slowly. He has a new black and white Buick Century, a two-door hardtop. I'll recognize it if I see it." His eyes dart and search each vehicle. Roger begins to perspire.

"He? Who's he? Who owns that Buick?" I open a fresh pack of Lucky Strike Cigarettes and light one up. The pack finds its way back to my pocket while I wait for an answer. I steer the car up and down each row. The lot is full.

"Sally's new boyfriend. A gang of couples are supposed to have some kind of big picnic here today. If I find him with her I'll break his neck." His eyes never stop moving. He frantically searches every inch of the grounds.

"You can't do that man. You said you broke up. That means the two of you don't go together anymore. It's over. She can go out with anyone. So can you. You're both footloose and fancy-free. I know it hurts, but that's the way it is. Put it behind you and get on with your life."

Either he hasn't heard me, or he doesn't want to hear me. At any rate I'm certain I didn't get through to him. We slowly pass each car. There is no Buick.

"Take that road over there" He points to it. "That takes you to a smaller lot on the other side of the park. Let's check that out."

I drive the route slowly. Two vehicles occupy the second lot, a pick-up truck with camper and a van. Beads of sweat fill his face. He looks at me. "They're not here. Let's go. Some people live in a tree. I live in a rotten log." Suddenly he goes through a transformation. A wild look comes over him. He screams at me, "DON'T TELL ME WHAT TO DO! YOU DIDN'T LOSE YOUR LADY! BESIDES, I SAVED THE CROWS DIDN'T I?" This time his voice has a hysterical cackle to it, one that reminds me of an evil witch. He lowers his head and sits, almost in tears.

I turn the car around and head for the entrance. Roger continues to act bizarre. He runs his hands up and down the dashboard and frantically searches it. He stops at the glove compartment lock and stares.

He depresses the round button and the small door falls open. He rummages through the interior and inspects every item until he finds my flashlight. He takes it out, returns the other articles, and slams the door shut. He tries the light. It works.

As we reach the entrance I point to the instruments "It's getting late, we're low on petrol buddy. How much money do you have?" I'm about to discover I've made a horrendous mistake. We're almost broke and out of gas.

Roger searches his pockets and turns them inside out. A few coins rest in the palm of his hand. He adds them," Twenty-six cents. I have twenty-six cents." He states the total proudly.

"Not pocket change. I'm talking about folding green, paper money."

"That's it. That's all I got. You guys cleaned me out yesterday." He sounds wounded "I don't even have a credit card."

I reach for my wallet. It's not there. I search the other pockets. My checkbook isn't there either; I finally realize the trousers I wore yesterday hang draped over a chair back in my room. My wallet, credit cards, money and checkbook are in those gabardine slacks.

I search the pockets of my hunting clothes. No luck. Don't I always keep some money in the watch pocket of my camouflage in case of an emergency? This certainly qualifies as one. My fingers dig deep into the cloth chamber and I feel them touch wadded up paper tightly wrapped around coins. I empty the pocket and unfold the green ball.

One crumpled up dollar bill and fourteen cents. Add the twenty-six cents Roger has, and our combined bankroll amounts to one dollar and forty cents. It helps, but not enough. Roger racks up the volume on the radio. He turns on the flashlight, presses it into the side of my face, and shines the beam of light directly in my right eye. Startled, and temporarily blinded, I knock the light aside and lower the radio.

Instinctively I begin to make a left turn out of the parking lot and retrace our steps. Roger pipes up "Wrong way man. Hang a right. There's a gas station a few miles up the road. We use it every time we come up here."

I am not familiar with the area so I make the right. Again, it's as if some undefined power guides me. I can't explain why, but I listen to Roger. The park is five miles behind us now and we haven't reached a gas station. Roger blares the radio, turns on the flashlight, presses it into the side of my face, and shines it in my eye.

I knock the light away for the second time and lower the volume. Suddenly an old enemy is back, fear, fear that creeps up from the gut. Fear because you know things are out of control. There is no rational way to explain what could happen next.

Roger exhales deeply, spins the light around, holds it by the bulb, lashes out, and strikes me across the side of my face with the body of the flashlight.

It catches me completely by surprise. I see stars for an instant. The side of my jaw feels as though it's on fire. I let out a yell, and retaliate. I throw a punch. My right hand lands solidly on Roger's head.

He recoils "What'd you hit me for?" His surprise is genuine.

If I don't realize the situation by now, I'm as crazy as he is "You hit me. I hit back. You better calm down. I didn't cause your break up. You did. I had enough of your nonsense. You better think of a way for us to get back home." I rub the soreness from my cheek and drive.

At last we spot a gas station. Not the one Roger said was there, but a very welcome sight. I put on the tum signal and slow down "Give me all the change you have. We need every penny for gas, and we're still not going to have enough to get home." The indicator now hovers just above empty.

"I'm not giving you my money! What are you trying to do, mug me? No way. I need my money." His eyes glaze over.

We pull in and a Station Attendant steps out "Fill it up sir?"

I signal for him to wait. The passenger door opens. Roger steps out and makes a beeline for the rest room. I put what money I have on the hood and count it. I thoroughly search my pockets for the second time and try to will money to appear. None docs. I ask the worker "How much is the cheapest?"

He cleans the windshield "Motor is 31 cents a gallon."

"Give me exactly one dollar and fourteen cents worth of the cheapest you got, and drain the hose."

The Attendant gives me an odd look, but does what I ask, and even drains the hose. Roger hasn't finished yet? I need to use the facilities myself and enter the rest room. Roger has the place in a mess. Every paper towel is pulled from the dispensers and lie randomly scattered around the room.

Each toilet paper roll is unrolled and strewn across the floor. Every faucet runs wide open. Roger continually flushes each urinal and commode "Some people live in a tree. I live in a rotten log." When I enter he brushes by me and leaves.

I shut the water off, pick up what papers I can, and make an attempt to straighten out the place. Outside, Roger and the Station Attendant stand at the coffee machine and argue.

"This machine sells coffee for forty cents a cup and I'm not lending you the difference." The attendant stands his ground. His statement falls on deaf ears. Roger is beyond understanding the price of a cup of coffee or anything else. I intervene and seat Roger in the automobile.

The Attendant watches "He looks nervous."

"He is. Check your men's room. I straightened it out a little, but check it anyway. I'm in a situation here. What's the shortest way to Pittsburgh?"

The man doesn't hesitate. He points "Straight ahead for twelve miles. You'll come to an intersection. Turn left at that light. That puts you on route twenty-two west. One hundred fifty seven miles down that road is Pittsburgh. Can you make it that far on four gallons of gas?"

I quickly do the arithmetic. My car averages sixteen miles to the gallon on a trip. There were about three gallons in the tank, add what we just bought, and we have close to seven gallons. Sixteen times seven...we can't make it. I shake my head no, and start the car

As we leave the station and I wonder how we're going to get back. It is five-thirty in the afternoon, and getting dark. We make it to Route twenty-two before I hear from my passenger again. At the intersection we wait for the light to change. Roger acts up. He shines the flashlight in my eye just as the signal turns green. Traffic starts to move. Almost blinded I keep up with the flow and somehow manage to make it through the tum. At last we head in the right direction.

Roger screams "SOME PEOPLE LIVE IN A TREE. I LIVE IN A ROTTEN LOG." In a rage he slides across the seat as far as his seatbelt lets him. He swings his foot over, positions it on top of mine, and stomps down as hard as he can. At the same time he grabs the steering wheel and won't let go.

The automobile leaps forward. My foot is pinned under his and on the accelerator, He throws the wheel as hard as he can to the left. We gain speed rapidly, cross the centerline, and head into oncoming traffic.

I hit him hard with a forearm and knock him back onto his side of the car. The force of the blow frees his hand from the wheel and I fight to get my foot out from under his. I kick him off me and somehow manage to get the car under control and back onto our side of the road without a collision. An oncoming trucker blares his horn and gives us the finger as he glides by. Someone definitely watches out for us.

Roger turns the radio up full blast. He grabs the steering wheel a second time and stomps on my foot "I SAVED THE CROWS," he screams and we rocket forward. We head toward the rear end of a station wagon immediately in front of us.

I kick hard with my left leg and knock his foot free. I put all the strength I can muster into a punch and launch it. It lands solidly. His hand rips free and he bangs against the passenger side, car door.

I stand on the brake with both feet and watch the station wagon come closer. Burning rubber fills the air. Tires screech. It's all I can do to hold us straight. The front- end dips. We skid, and stop, inches away from the rear of the wagon. Surrounding motorists lay on their horns and curse us.

"Damn! You trying to kill us? I don't know if I can take a hundred and fifty miles of this." I lower the radio.

My words reach Roger. He calms doom, at least for a while. He lights up another Marlboro, and I have my second Lucky Strike. We smoke in silence. The next thirty miles pass without flare-ups. That's fine with me.

The fuel gauge drops below a quarter tank. We have a hundred and twenty miles to go and it's almost dark. I turn the headlights on low beams. Just when I begin to hope I can relax Roger starts again "Some people live..." he's back from where ever he was. I feel my muscles grow tense. On full alert, I anticipate what's next, and try to plan how to deal with it. Time is not on my side.

His eyes glaze over. A wild look crosses his face. He frantically searches the automobile interior with those crazed eyes and sweats. He turns the radio on full blast, lunges across the seat and shuts off the headlights. He stomps down on my foot, and again grabs the steering wheel. We roar down the highway in the dark. A brightly lit, tractor-trailer truck approaches in the opposite lane. The distance between us closes rapidly. Roger has my foot pinned under his.

He forces the wheel hard to the left and keeps a death grip on it. We accelerate and fly directly into the path of the oncoming truck. This time we're not so lucky.

I fight for my life and finally manage to knock Roger's hand free from the wheel. There's no room to maneuver and get safely back on our side of the road. The distance between our vehicles vanishes. We can't survive a head on collision. I have no choice. I keep the car floored, steer at an angle that carries us directly into the path of the truck, and shoot across the macadam.

Our car leaves the road surface and goes onto the soft shoulder between the oncoming truck and the guardrails. His air horn pierces the night and blares continuously. He narrowly misses us. The car rocks as the trailer slips by.

I regain the gas pedal, stand on the brake, and throw the wheel hard to the right. The rear end starts to slide. There is a sickening crunch of metal. The car vibrates violently. We sideswipe the guardrail, maintain contact with it, and slide along its length. I fight desperately to control the automobile.

A shower of hot sparks erupts from the barrier and fills the air near my face. I flashback and think of another time the air was full of deadly red dots. Korea 1952. Marine Technical Sergeant Russell holds his M 1 rifle high and screams "INCOMINGI

I-HIT THE DECK!" The two of us dive for cover and land in a hole a jumble of tangled of arms and legs.

The Sergeant somehow lands on top of me and our faces are inches apart. His flaming red handle bar moustache is covered with mud and ice hangs from it. His cheeks are dotted with small white circles, one under each eye, the signs of frostbite. He speaks directly into my face "Well jarhead, you wanted action, you got it." Tufts and clumps of snow covered frozen dirt kick loose above us. Small fingers of hot red fill the air and a spray of icy soil splatters over everything.

We scramble to free ourselves from each other, and return fire. Sergeant Russell continues "Never let your buddy down no matter how rough it gets, or what it costs. If you do, just about the time you need your buddy, he'll let you down." We stayed alive by honoring those words then. I live by them now, and always will.

Heavy vibrations from the steering wheel return me to the present. I am not carrying a rifle. I am struggling to regain control of an automobile. We slow down and that allows me to steer away from the guardrail, cross the highway, and get back onto our side of the asphalt.

Vehicles pass. They sound their horns, blink their lights, and shout obscenities at us. I'm grateful we are able to hear the curses. I find an opening in traffic, get in the curbside lane, search for a clear spot, pull off the road, and stop "Do you realize what you just did? What almost happened?"

Roger smiles, pulls another Marlboro from his almost empty pack, and lights up." My tree may be a rotten log, but at least I saved the crows."

I fire up a Lucky. We sit and smoke. I turn the radio down and am amazed how calm I am. My mind makes split second decisions. My body reacts to every threat, and yet through it all I manage to maintain control. Roger settles down, but only for a moment. He smokes non-stop. Further attempts to reason with him will be fruitless. I don't even try.

His outbursts cost us precious fuel. I notice the gas gauge. I buckle Roger's seatbelt. He doesn't resist. At least it restricts his movement somewhat, maybe enough to allow me to continue.

I restart the car and slip it into drive. The Highway Patrol passes but doesn't stop. I wait for an opening and pull into traffic. Roger stares straight ahead and mumbles incoherently. He turns on the flashlight and shines it in my eye. He shuts off the headlights, I turn them on, he blares the radio, I lower it, I knock the light aside; he immediately puts it back in my face. We ride this way for the next fifty miles.

I discover a way to position my foot so he can't pin it to the accelerator. I rest the toe of my boot on the hump in the center of the floorboard that covers the transmission and use my heel to depress the pedal. It is an extremely awkward and uncomfortable position, but when I consider the alternatives I gladly tolerate the inconvenience'

Roger winces "Some people live in a tree. I live in a rotten log." He crumples his now empty cigarette pack into a ball and tosses it out the window. He searches his pockets and panics "I'm out of cigarettes." His words fall somewhere between a whimper, and a cry.

I offer him mine "Smoke a decent cigarette for once. Have a Lucky."

He's offended by the suggestion and gently pushes my hand aside "A Lucky? How can anyone smoke those weeds? I want a real cigarette, a king size, filtered, Marlboro."

"You're out, you smoked them all. Look in the ashtray. Maybe you left a good sized butt in there. It's either that, or have a Lucky."

He slides the tray open and when he does I hear a distinct sound of metal contacting metal. Suddenly he changes his mind and slams the door closed. There's that sound again "A butt!" He's offended by the suggestion "I want a real cigarette, not a butt. Pull in somewhere. I'll buy a pack."

Sure he will. We pass a road sign, Pittsburgh, fifty-three miles. I read the gauge and it's just above empty. We'll never make it. Another sign comes into view. This one is a billboard that advertises a roadside diner, one of those places that used to be a railroad car but was remodeled and made over into a restaurant. It's a mile ahead.

Roger kicks viciously at the floor. "I want a Marlboro." He searches himself again. The lights from the diner come into view. I put on the turn signals and slow down. I'm glad to see they have a gas station. Several tractor-trailer trucks and a few vehicles dot the lot. The gas pumps are in use. They're open. Good. We pull in and park.

Before I get the motor shut off Roger loosens his seatbelt, climbs out, runs, and enters the diner. I turn my attention elsewhere. I remove the ashtray completely, carry it outside, put my hand over the opening, and turn it upside down.

Ashes and cigarette butts fall between my fingers but I hold onto the metal that made the clinking sounds, loose change I forgot was there. I sweep away the remaining dirt, and count. Thirty-five cents in coins, I put the ashtray back in and follow Roger into the restaurant. Cigarettes out of a machine cost more than thirty-five cents a pack, damn! I had hoped there would have been enough for him to at least get his Marlboros, anything to keep him quiet. I shake my head. Through the window I can see Roger. He stands at the counter, gestures, and waves his hands about.

Customers and waitresses watch him. He uses his forearm to clear away part of the counter top nearest him. Condiments fall to the floor as he sweeps that section clean. "Deal Omaha! Seven handed! Two dollar, four dollar! Hey houseman, bring me a pack of king size, filtered, Marlboro Cigarettes."

He sees me, stops what he's doing, and retreats to the restrooms. The commotion has everyone's attention. A light comes from a door nicked away in the rear of the place and marked "Office." I follow Roger to the lavatory. He brushes by me and makes a beeline for the counter.

Voices filter through to me, but I can't quite make out what is being said. I exit the room, and walk toward the counter. A waitress stands across from Roger. Her order pad and pencil poised, she writes as he speaks.

"I want a large T-bone steak, medium well, mashed potatoes, gravy on the mashed, a tossed salad with vinegar and oil, hot rolls with butter, coffee, one cream, one sugar, and a glass of water. Bring me a pack of king size, filtered, Marlboro cigarettes, and a fresh deck of cards." I pick up the fallen condiments and place them on the counter.

The waitress turns to me "Miss, don't fill that order. We have no money. We can't pay for that food."

Roger continues "Top it off with a large piece of blueberry pie and a scoop of vanilla ice cream, and give him the check." Roger points to me "He's loaded. He kills for money."

Customers nearby hear the remark, pick up, and quietly move away. Roger continues," Bang. Ten cents. Bang. Ten cents. Every time he shoots the cash register rings, and mine's all gone, girls gone, money's gone, cigarettes gone, birds are gone, everything's gone." His head sags for a moment.

I interrupt, "I would like to speak with your boss, or the manager, or whoever is in charge. Would you please call them out here?"

Roger Rambles on, "Where are my Marlboros?"

The waitress sees I am serious. She rips the page off her order pad, crumples it into a ball, and discards it. She heads for the office and I go to the vending machine. The large red sticker reads, Cigarettes four dollars a pack, all brands. I deposit the coins – all thirty five cents worth before realizing that this would be a futile exercise. Nothing happens, of course, so I walk back to Roger.

"I made a mistake. I didn't have enough money. I realized it after I started depositing the change. Sorry." I really was trying to get him a fresh pack. My explanation is wasted.

He screams, "DAMNIT GENE! I WANT KING SIZE, FILTERED, MARLBORO CIGARETTES, NOT SOME DAMN EXCUSE, WHO SAVED THE CROWS?"

"Just relax, Roger." I reached in and pulled out my pack of Luckies to at least offer him something. "Maybe this will work—"

He makes an unexpected move. He swats the hand that holds the pack and knocks it free. The cigarettes sail across the aisle and land near the booted foot of a trucker who sits nearby.

This man has been watching us since we came in. He leans forward in his chair, reaches down, and picks up the fallen smokes. He hands them to me. "You two driving a late model dark colored car?"

I take the pack. "Thank you. How'd you know that?"

He ignores my question. "Are you traveling west on twenty two?"

He surprises me with the remark. "Yes. How do you know that?"

He continues, "Did you have a close call with a big rig a few miles back?"

Now I am curious. "Yeah. How is it you know that?"

He explains. "The latest thing. Most truckers now have C.B. Radios, the air been buzzing about you. Everybody figures you must be drunk, but I see you're not. You in trouble? You need help?"

I motion toward Roger. "He has a problem." I point to my head and spin my finger. "I'm trying to get him, get both of us, home, alive. He tries to wreck the car while I drive. I think we can make it if I can get some gas."

The trucker responds, "Call the State Police. Let them handle him. It'll be safer for you, and for everyone else on the road."

I consider his suggestion and reject it." No. No cops. It would embarrass his family and cost them a lot of money they don't have."

We look at each other. His reply makes sense. "Better embarrassed than dead. What about other motorists? The innocent victims you might take with you if you don't make it. No. I think you should call the police. They're trained to deal with situations like this, and if they can't handle it, they know where to get the help, and right now, and from the people who do know."

Again I rule against him. "I know you're right but I can't call the police on him. We'll make it, somehow."

The trucker reaches in his shirt and produces a newly opened pack of king size, filtered, Marlboros. He hands them to me. "Here, I'll trade you these for the Luckies. At least it might calm him down a little."

I thank him, make the trade, and hand the pack of filters to Roger. He attacks it. He lights up and drags deeply. It does calm him.

The manager steps behind the counter and approaches, "Yes. You wish to see me? Is anything wrong with your food? What's the problem?" He stands back and is irritated. We interrupted his work.

I look straight into his eyes. "We're from a small town just outside of Pittsburgh. The problem is we're broke, and we're out of gas. The tank is on empty and we can't make it home. We don't even have a credit card. We need you to trust us for a tank of gas, and if you could see your way clear, two cups of coffee."

The manager notices a nervous Roger, he looks at my clothes and his attitude changes. He relaxes. "You seem to have more than one problem. I'll call the police for you. That I can do."

Roger hears the word police and begins to tremble. He breaks into a sweat and drags deeply on his cigarette. His hands shake as though he were palsied.

I nod in the direction of the seated driver. "That trucker over there suggested the same thing. I can't do that. What we really need is a tank of gas and a couple cups of coffee."

The manager looks at Roger again, then back to me, "You have no money at all? Nothing?" He thinks for a moment. "Do you have anything you can put up as collateral? A camera? A dress coat? Anything?"

Roger lights another cigarette. "I saved the crows from this killer. That should be worth something."

Reluctantly, I concede, "In the trunk of my car I have an Ithaca, Featherlight, twelve gauge, pump action, shotgun, and a bag of shells. I'd rather not leave that, but if I have to I will. You give me a written receipt. I'll be out here first thing tomorrow, pay what I owe, and get it back."

The manager appraises the situation. He sizes me up. He probably thinks I'm as crazy as Roger. He makes a decision. "No gums. I don't want yours, or any weapons in here. We have a large turnover in hired help and I wouldn't trust it lying around, not even if it's only overnight. Someone might steal it. Use pump number five, and get your gas." He turns to the waitress. "Give them two cups of coffee."

I return and a steaming brew is set in front of me. The manager hands me a piece of paper. "You must have been running on fumes. It took twenty-four gallons. That comes to seventy five for gas, plus two dollars for the two coffees. I expect payment in full for the total. Our business address, and my name, is printed on the back of the receipt. No need for you to make a special trip, mail it in. I still think you should call the police. Good luck." He retires to his office.

Roger hears police mentioned again and gets very nervous. He finishes the rest of his coffee in one gulp, lights another Marlboro, gets up, and steps outside.

I read the address and enjoy the coffee. I fold the receipt and tuck it in my shirt pocket. I notice headlights reflect off the glass ease behind the counter. That's strange. There's another set. Horns blare wildly and tires screech, that's odd.

I never noticed those reflections before. Suddenly I'm on full alert. "Where's Roger?" I quickly finish the brew, thank the waitress, and hurry out the door.

I don't see him at first. A squeal of tires catches my attention. A car swerves wildly and blares its horn. The glow from automobile headlights frame Roger in silhouette. He is in the center of the highway.

His arms are askew. He wobbles. He walks the painted centerline as though he is doing a balancing act on a high wire. Heel to toe he traverses the double yellow stripe.

Traffic from both directions veers sharply to avoid hitting him. Tears stream down his cheeks and he screams. "SOME PEOPLE LIVE IN A TREE. I LIVE IN A ROTTEN LOG."

I run out onto the road and catch up to him. He throws punches at an imaginary foe. I grab his arm. He rips free. "THE CROW KILLER IS HERE. BETTER WATCH OUT."

This time I forcefully grab him. Another car narrowly misses us. I lead him off the road, get him in the car, and fasten his seatbelt. I securely close and lock his door.

I get in. The gauge reads full. The tank of gas eases my tension. I hurriedly hide the flashlight by wedging it between the seats and start the car. I turn on the headlights and pull out. I estimate we have less than an hour before we're home. I fail to prop my foot to protect the accelerator and this momentary lapse in concentration will prove to nearly cost us our lives.

Roger sits and smokes. His face contorts. He finds the light and pulls it free. He turns the radio on and blares it. He puts the light in my eye. I feel my body react and get tense. Another road sign shows Pittsburgh is twenty miles away.

A short distance ahead is a natural gas company pumping station. The grounds are brightly lit. The facility is on our side of the road. The entire perimeter is enclosed with cyclone fence that stands eight feet high. The lawn is manicured. Large pipes and several white painted buildings stand out even in the dark.

Something else awaits us. Another tractor-trailer. It too, is headed for Pittsburgh, Amber lights outline the rear of the vehicle and appear to grow larger the closer we get. I knock the flashlight aside. The distance shrinks.

Roger reacts. He goes completely berserk. He reaches over and shuts off the headlights, he blares the radio, crushes my foot under his, grabs the steering wheel, and screams, "NOW CROW KILLER, HOW DO YOU LIKE IT?"

I fight for my life and repeatedly punch his hand and kick his foot. We gain speed. He aims us straight at the rear of the truck. Our two thousand pound rocket hurtles forward. We reach a speed of seventy-five miles an hour. I call on every ounce of strength I can muster, coil my left leg and launch it at his foot

At last I manage to kick his foot free and knock it back on his side of the car. He cries out in pain. I cup my hands together and use both arms as a club. I swing at the hand that clutches the steering wheel, and with my full force I manage to hit his wrist.

His grip breaks and his hand rips free. I hit him a second time and knock him back on his own side of the seat.

The car flies toward the truck. I put two feet on the brake and stand on the pedal. The automobile's front end dips sharply. We go under the rear of the tractor-trailer. I exert all the force on the brake I can muster. They squeal in protest. We hit into the large rubber mud flap that hangs just under the back of the truck bed.

I throw the steering wheel to the right. We manage to miss the rear tires by fractions of an inch and fly out from underneath the trailer compartment. How we avoid a collision is beyond explanation and can only carry one interpretation, "Somebody up their watches out for us."

We're not out of danger yet. The car leaves the highway at sixty miles an hour. We carom off the roadside barrier. I force the wheel to the left and continue to stand on the brake. At fifty-miles an hour we skid sideways and slam into the guardrails. We slide along the cables in another shower of sparks, this time from the passenger side.

Crunching metal accompanies the fireworks. We maintain contact with the barrier until it ends. Tires burn and brakes scream. We finally come to a full stop in the center of the driveway that is the main entrance to the Gas Company Plant. I don't have time to relax.

Roger leaps from the car, runs to the front gate, and tries to force his way inside. It is locked. He climbs up, crawls over the fence, and illegally enters the pump station. He runs across the lawn and heads in the direction of the largest white building.

I tum off the ignition, leave the car in the driveway entrance, and start to climb. I'm over the fence, and clear of the gate when a voice booms out from behind me, "HOLD IT RIGHT THERE MISTER! DON'T YOU MOVE!" The sound of glass breaking in the distance interrupts the Plant Guard.

It comes from the direction of a large building. He glances toward that area then turns back to me. "WHAT'S GOING ON HERE?"

We face each other. "I climbed your fence. So did the guy that's with me. I think we just heard from him. He's sick, a mental case. I'm trying to get him home. Help me."

Wood shattering and splintering make up his mind. Together, the two of us run toward the noise. "This other guy. What's he doing?"

I pant from the exertion, "Beats me."

We approach the building and the Guard turns on his flashlight. Its beam pierces the shadows and illuminates the entranceway. Dirt, broken glass, and splinters of white painted wood litter the sidewalk. What used to be a planter lies scattered about. Remnants of the flowers it once held form a haphazard pattern that dots the debris.

The door is ajar. Slivers of glass that used to be a window cling to what's left of a frame. Tom remains of flowers hang suspended from those glass chards. The Guard slowly forces the door open. More broken planter pieces, dirt, glass, and flowers inside are shoved out of the way to allow the door to swing wide. We enter with caution.

We stand on spotless, highly polished, floors. Our eyes search the clean walkways and aisles. The place glistens. Everything is clean and free of clutter.

We stare through a maze of scaffolding-like polished steel beam structures erected to reinforce and support each massive gas pipe and try to figure where to start looking.

Suddenly a voice comes from above. "Caw, Caw. I live in a rotten log."

The Guard and I regard one another for a second, then at the same time, look up. Roger sits in the overhead some thirty feet above. He waves his arms as though he has wings. His legs dangle over the side of one of the large pipes. He uses it as a seat. His arms wrap around steel braces and he leans his chest against the cross members. He looks down at us from his perch and grins.

The Guard issues me an order. "Keep your eye on him. I'll call the police."

I plead. "Please. No police. He's not a criminal, he's sick. We can get him down and out of here." I sense the Guard trusts me. He looks up at Roger then studies the superstructure.

He makes a decision. "You climb the right side." He points, "I'll take this one. We'll have him between us and he'll have no way out. Do you think he'll jump?"

I shake my head no, and begin to climb. Roger sits and watches us. He nods approval as we gain height. He is amused and our feat of mountaineering seems to entertain him. We make it to the level he sits on and converge on him. The Guard reaches him first. I'm only a step behind. Roger can't get away.

We take hold of him and a strange thing happens. Roger relaxes completely. It's almost as though he is relieved we're here. He offers no resistance.

The Guard inspects the area for damages and the three of us descend in order. I take the lead, Roger is sandwiched between us, and the Guard climbs last.

Safely on the floor, Roger's demeanor changes. He becomes a helpless whipped puppy, and almost childishly, says, "When I'm gone who will save the crows?"

The Guard is convinced. I explain the situation while we lead Roger across the grounds. I get him back in the car. The Guard copies my license plate, takes our names, and describes the automobile.

"This isn't the last of it. I am required to report the incident. I will write up a complete statement and relate the events. Bringing charges of illegal entry, trespass, and destruction of company property is a supervisory decision. I'm almost certain they will demand full restitution for all damages. I will make a statement in your behalf. I'll explain the situation, the condition of your friend, and your circumstances. How it will affect their decision I can't say. Maybe you'll have to answer for it, maybe you won't. That's up to them. Good luck."

The Guard locks the gate. I thank him again and get back on the road. Roger has a Marlboro going and I light up a Lucky. Traffic builds as we approach the city. A street sign tells us our exit is one mile ahead. I put on the turn signal, make a lane change, and slow down for the off ramp. Roger reaches over and turns on the radio.

This time it plays at a normal level. Just like that, it is over. It is as though someone threw a switch and made a dark room light. A different person sits there. He talks quietly.

The hysteria is gone. "Gene, I never should have bet my pair of deuces into that ace, queen, ten, of hearts." He refers to a play he made in the poker game. "That hand cost me some bread."

At last I feel I can relax. "It's not good poker Roger, you know that. You should have dropped, or checked into him. At least that way you get to see if he has a weak hand, or if he steps out and bets."

"That hand cost me my last forty-eight dollars. All I got out of it was a cold ham sandwich and a stale cup of coffee. That's high priced vittles." He laughs. "You guys chopped me up and had me for lunch."

The remainder of the trip is uneventful. We finally pull up in front of his house. I accompany him to his front door, wait until he is safely inside, hear the door lock click shut, and see lights go on.

At the hotel I sit parked and say a quiet prayer of thanks while I have a cigarette. I am grateful we survived. Under the glow of the streetlight I examine my automobile. The damages are extensive and I'm certain they will be worse in daylight, but then I consider the alternatives.

I get the shotgun and shells out of the trunk and head for my room. The trousers I wore yesterday hang draped over the chair. I take out my wallet, find an envelope in a desk drawer, write a brief note, and stuff some money in it. I seal it, put a stamp on it, and lay it on top of the desk.

Under the covers I'm suddenly exhausted. I fall asleep almost immediately.

"GENE KARNES! GET UP! IT'S ME! PAUL DANTZ! ROGERS' BROTHER! OPEN THE DOOR! WE HAVE TO TALK TO YOU!"

The pounding doesn't let up. I guess it runs in the family. I get out of bed, pull on a robe, and open the door.

Paul, and a Person I've never seen before stand in the hall. The Stranger wears a quietly understated, elegant, and very expensive suit. He carries both an attaché case and a portable machine that I can't quite see because Paul blocks my view. I invite them in.

The older man sits at the desk. He shoves aside my sealed, stamped, envelope addressed to a diner, and sets his portable machine down. He plugs a small microphone into its side, puts in a fresh cassette tape, depresses the record button, and speaks into the mike. "First interview with Gene Kames in regard to Roger Dantz." He adds the day, time, and date, shuts the machine off, rewinds it, and plays it back.

Satisfied, he turns the contraption off, opens his attaché case, removes a thick legal pad, and several pencils.

Paul adds, "We know you were with my brother Roger yesterday. We had to commit him to the psychiatric ward at St. Francis Hospital five-thirty this morning. This is Doctor Walters. He is Rogers' psychiatrist. We want you to answer some questions about you and my brother. Where you went? What you did? How'd he behave? Was he acting odd? That sort of thing."

The Doctor positions the pad, picks up a pencil, and turns on the recorder. "I couldn't help but notice your automobile. It has sustained considerable damage. How did that happen? We'd like for you to recount the time you spent with Roger yesterday and in your own words tell us what you did, and what happened Anything you recall could be important, no matter how insignificant. It is just possible you may have witnessed him cross the line from sanity to insanity. Just speak clearly into the microphone."

I fight my conscience. Am I about to betray a friend? Violate a trust? Should I remain silent, or speak up?

Paul's eyes answer those questions for me. He is desperate. He searches frantically for any way to help his brother. His eyes plead for explanations, and answers. Paul asks, "And what's all this business about how he saved the crows?

THE END

ABOUT THE AUTHOR

George Kosana starred as Sheriff McClelland in the horror classic *The Night of the Living Dead*, and delivered the famous ad-lib line, "They're dead! They're all messed up."

He played an abortionist's front man in George Romero's follow-up movie, *The Affair*, which was a romantic comedy. He continued his acting career with roles in *The Booby Hatch*, *The Devil and Sam Silverstein*, and three other independent films. Still active in the entertainment business, he delights his many fans when he appears at horror conventions for autograph signings throughout The United States.

George is an accomplished writer as well as an actor. His original screenplay *We'll Try Again*, won the Silver Award at the Houston International Film Festival. George's current project *Madness, Times Three* deals with three distinctly different psychological disorders, of which this story, *Save the Crows* is the first part.

His short story *Tiffany's!! It's Get Even Time!!* appears in *The Big Book of Bizarro* by Burning Bulb Publishing.